Saladin's Sword

A
PAPAL
TREASURE
PART 2 -
THE SECRET
OF THE
SCRIMSHAW
THE CAPTAIN'S
LOG BOOK

JAMES JONES

BALBOA.
PRESS

A DIVISION OF HAY HOUSE

Balboa Press books may be ordered through booksellers or by contacting:

Balboa Press
A Division of Hay House
1663 Liberty Drive
Bloomington, IN 47403
www.balboapress.com.au
1 (877) 407-4847

Print information available on the last page.

ISBN: 978-1-4525-3024-6 (sc)
ISBN: 978-1-4525-3025-3 (e)

Balboa Press rev. date: 03/29/2016

Contents

A Papal Treasure
Part 2

Chapter 1

andetta lay just outside an inlet,with a strong northly wind blowing into the small bay. Captain de villier studied his navigation chart,for any hazards around the island of cidros off the coast of mexico. the fleet of pirate vessels waited for,the 900 ton spanish galleon matador,commanded by admirale don alfrdeo guanti.he had served in wars,against england and france.de villier heard shouting above,and went up on deck to see several men instructing groups of men around each.the big zulu koonah,showed them the art of unarmed combat.which parts of the body to hit,to cause the most damage or kill if necessary.a small oriental chap,quong gee reached down,into a large wooden box the armourer had put in front of him on a keg.he took out 5 circular throwing knives,chose one and threw it hard to his right. A wild yell was heard,as a silver blur took a seaman,s hat off then a thunk was heard and a pitch screech as the knife embbeded into nelson.s neck.as nelson was the crews favourite cat,the men gasped in horror and diago ran to tell the captain of this gruesome murder.diago returned with a bundle,in his arms,and whispered to quong gee.attension men your young midshipman has a talent,as a breeder of cats and has a surpise for you.diago stood on a box,to be at eye level,with the men.he opened the bundle,and there sat a grey persian kitten with white paws.gentlemen the captain has named this great tiger horatio tuppence.nelson was his father and petunia,the cat chavez owns is his mother,so nelson lives on.then diago said,he held up a gold chain with an engraved tag attached,he said, this gold chain is part of the treasure,from the first spanish galleon and the captain has promoted tuppence to 4th leftenant,from rat catcher, a great cheer went up,from the crew. I am not very happy,as tuppence now out ranks me as a midshipman. the crew had a good laugh,and returned to there training.the two pirate captians,smthye jones and de villier.were chatting to captain van derman,from his vessel burgen anchored nearby.he told them of his visit to to the ambassador,at el salvador an old friend,whom he supplies chocolates,and fine cuban cigars.a special order on every voyage. pablo a tall bronzed skinned man.said we have made a plan,and handed captian jones a rolled parchment and an envelope.my brother is an architect senor,and spent many hours creating all the fine details.muchas grasias captain jones said,and unrolled the parcment,putting weights on each corner.diago please open the safe,and give pablo 50 gold dubloons to share with his brother,for good service rendered.santana said,we have enough room for 600 men and supplies,on our fishing boats and canoes captain.there is 210 ten men as crew on the spanish galleon.de villier filled all,the glasses with fresh brandy for those present,then said gentlemen how many men are there at fort jurez,and in the township,this we must know.ten men guard the armoury,and five guard the powder magazine.santana was the headman of the local native village.he and 4 senior elders from 8 local villages,had come aboard to discuss plans to attack the matador and the fort at jurez.the spanish have been very cruel and harsh,with all my people senor capitano. We wish to get rid of them,once and for all.we have many strong men of all ages,some have been soldiers in wars with mexico and spain.most of the men have not been to war.our villages have many boats and canoes and we even have a large sloop,we captured from the french swine.we use this vessel,to trade with other tribes along the coast. We need pistols and rifles,ammunition and some small cannons for self defense capitano jones.the spanish dogs,raid all the villages,and take young men and women for slave labour or for the pleasure of the spanish officers.my own second daughter lima was kidnapped a week ago,as she washed clothes at the river.my friends caught the drunken officers,and slit there throats.65 men and women work and live in the fort at jurez.my men on shore will act as guides for your sailors,all the men of salinas are at your service.we want the commandante of the fort,colonel miguel de vinto,captured alive to go on public trial for henious crimes over the last 6 years,cortez do you have plenty of your magic voodoo powder,s left to use on the spanish officers.15 senior men in all,at dinner a meal they shall never forget said captian de villier.si capitano 3 of my men will visit the kitchens at the fort,and drug the food,wine and water.said colonel cortez. good that point is setteled,now we load all the boats and canoes just before sunset.chavez and santana go in first,with cortez and his crew dressed in spanish uniforms of soldiers and marines.chang will empty the amoury on shore,and set up his fire works.captian jones 2nd leftenant will act out his part,in the arrest of the spanish captain of the matador galleon.he and all his men,will be wearing yellow scarfes,so make no mistakes gentlemen by shooting one of your own men.all the boats were loaded and set sail for the fort.sancho and his band of cuthroats were put ashore,out of sight of the wharf and went on there way.the fat ugly pigs of spanish officers were scoffing huge amounts of spiked food and drinks and then coffee.koonah and quong with 40 men,there faces blackened,in dark clothes silently cut the throats of the spanish guards.they were on duty at 3 entrances to fort jurez.they crept inside,and chained all the doors shut to the barracks where the soldiers lived.the local staff,told them where all the other soldiers were on duty.koonah heard the sound of a blast and opened a nearby window.koonah saw rockets exploding above the ship quong use the pistols and grenades now,we need to clear all the rooms,arrest all the officers and dump them in wagons to take to the church,then the village council will take them for trial at a secret place. I will have all the men here killed and all the food and valubles taken away.the three villas next door to the fort were attacked and all the officers shot,or stabbed.the huge exotic food supply,shipped in by the governor was shared out equally to the population by wagon and mules in the coming weeks.on a flat piece of ground near a long jetty, a group of pirates were loading arms and ammo into large fishing boats.all the shocking tools of torture used by the inquisition dogs of the church,was loaded onto wagons to the matador and sunk with the vessel.many large canoes,had crept up at night on the bow and stern of matador. the men had grappling irons to hook on to the

Chapter 2

Vessel as soon as the fireworks started. each man was armed with a variety of weapons,plus a sachel of grenades with long wicks, a small hidden brazier was set up,in the middle of each canoe.the second men climbing up the rope,took rope ladders with them. these they tied to the deck rail,after the grenades were thrown at the spanish crew aboard .as this was occuring cortez with his men,came along the jetty and boarded the galleon matador.he screamed out,the fort is being attacked capitano generale. admiral don de santos,was already very angry, about the fireworks.then cortez showed him the arrest warrant for treason. Admiral santos said this is ridiculous who are you swine and where is your vessel,i have not been informed of any spanish warsihps in these seas.you impudent dog. the 6 senior spanish officers had been surrounded by cortez,s men,and stabbed 3 seaman at the stern of the galleon.they loaded and swung four swivel mounted carronades towards the officers on the quarterdeck.chavez and cortez with 100 men aimed there weapons at the spanish officers. lay down your swords and pistols,or you die now admiral,see the carronades poitnted at your men.a shot from a carronade killed 2 officers.grenades were exploding around the deck,killing 100s of spanish crew men.cortez shot the admiral in the head twice and the officers surrended.the crew fought on,until 265 men died,and 30 natives then captain de villier ordered a cease fire.32 pirates dead and 15 wounded was the battle toll.all the spanish crew left,were locked up in fort jurez. captian smythe jones had the carpenters and sailing masters inspect the matador completely from stem to stern for damage.all the dead were buried and the wounded cared for by the ships doctors and local nurses.the huge scottish bosun connolly,arrived a t he run to inform captain de villier he had found a 4 masted barque the cormorant,which was moored at a wharf behind the fort.only four senties,drunk as skunks on british rum from the holds, they was. said the bosun.diago told the captain,the vessle was capture a year ago,and santana said there were 125 british crew working in a gold mine in the hills.we bought them back to the hospital for to the matador captain.very good now organise a crew for both ships and see to food water and shot supplies.captian jones scoured the whole town,and surrounding area,for any deserters.he found 3 men hiding in a barn.he had them burned at the stake.the cormorant and galleon were repaired,and made sail a week later.the local natives were left with tons of weapons and shot,plus many chests of gold and jewels, 30 pirates stayed behind to train the natives to use weapons and tactics of warfare. captain jones would pick them up on his return voyage to england.the british crew were dropped off at panama,and the pirate fleet sailed south.john henry was the captain of the cormarant and was glad to be off the vessel beside de villier in his cabin.

he told a sad tale,of cheating and embezzlement by lord dunhill and his staff.the greedy fat pig,had 2 brothers in the admiralty and many shady deals had been done for years.lord dunhill had bought parts of the estates on captain jones and de villier. Special log books were used to record all these details,and many others.why where who,how and when needed to be known,to exact full retribution later.the two pirate captians at dinner,one evening,a good experienced captain is needed to visit the simpson bay dockyards on the virgin islands.you must superise the completion of a new 50 gun frigate of italian design,for the duke de montrief. john henry signed a contract,and was given 2 chests of gold dubloons and all the ships papers and log book. A number of forged documents, letters of marque,vatican ultima secret papers were handed over,with instructions on how and when to use them. when the ship was finished,and tested at sea,captian henry would sail for england with the treasure captured so far.at dover he would meet captain montoya to plan the next royal raid.back on the coast of south america,the 5 ships were waiting,as the crews saw 4 large barges sunk, to block the entrance to salinas inlet. chang and koonah had set the charges to blow the vessels up.three cutters with full crews,were rowing the two men back to there ship.they had found some useful equipment aboard the barges.siganl flags went up,the mast of vandetta,as de villier ordered more sail set.she picked up speed to sixteen knots as the wind caught her sails full on from a strong southerly breeze.it had been agreed,the swordfish and the jackal would escort the mississipi the new stern plate name for the spanish galleon.the deck had been altered to look like a american merchant ship and she flew the rebel flag of the southern states vandetta and alverado sailed far ahead,to check any enemy ships and were lost to sight from the deck.2 days later as the two ships were keeping pace,with the mississpi a sail was sighted astern by the lookout aboard jackal.within a short time,a norwegain merchant vessel of 60 guns was seen,a barque very sleek and fast.it came up along side swordfish the oslo was the ships name, and through his loudhailer captain yurgen shouted,captain jones you rouge,you have two french frigates coming up from astern.they want your head on a pike,they say very angry chaps indeed.will you run,or make a decent fight of it whato.permission to come aboard and discuss tactics sir.captain smythe jones ordered his bosun to heave too,and shouted back .permission granted captian,you are an irish vessel not norwegian and i know that voice well.he said call me a bloody rouge you yankee theiveing no account landlubber.

both vessels heaved too,and captain james boone was rowed to the swordfish,as he came on deck,he took a 12inch throwing knife from a seathe tied behind his neck.the bosun and captian jones were sharing a large water melon.as bosun connolly picked up a piece of melon boone,threw the knife and grabbed another from his right boot and threw that knife too.the first teledo knife took the new fedora hat off the bosun,s head and embedded into the mainmast with a thunk.the bosun dropped his piece of melon in suprise,and captain jones laughed out loud as he saw this,then felt something hit his chest.he looked down and there,was the second knife up to the hilt,in his tooled leather powder horn.still up to your old tricks james, how are you cousin,hale hearty and rich captain jones said.after being taught by a master in the circus.practise is essential besides a silent method of killing a man comes in handy,dont you agree.the bosun was still upset,and advanced on captain boone with a huge club made of hard ebony

Chapter 3

ood.he raised it above his head and said,lets be havin ya,no one throws a wee knife at me and gets away with it yankee captian boone hit the bosun hard in the throat,and knocked him flat.the doctor was called and the bosun taken away.to my cabin now boone,before any more trouble occurs on deck.as the two captains were sipping spanish madeira,james boone said the french frigates are the cherbourge 45 guns,and nantes 50 guns.i met both captains of the,évessels when i called in for supplies and fresh water at panama.captian fecampe and rouscott,two men of vast experience of war at sea,both against england and spain.i was informed of a spanish treasure

galleon,that has gone off course,or disappeared.a course for ecuador is where the french,will sail checking any suspicious vessels along the way.we are good friends,as i often sail into there home port of brest for trading purposes.my barque is repaired and careened at the dry dock there.there was a knock at the cabin door,and captian jones called enter.cortez and sancho came into the cabin,cortez said you heave to capitano what is the reason sir.we have two hunters after our blood cortez,well armed french frigates and extremely dangerous to our grand plan. We have options,so lets sit and discuss them now,as we dont have much time before the ships arrive.replied captian jones.well we can run to shore and hide the ships in a bay .i know well. we can take the galleon up the river,and pretend we seek shelter to make repairs to our ships.two rivers flow into the bay at pisco.sancho showed the men,present the location of the bay on a chart of peru.sancho pointed out the location on the chart,his finger was on the trujillo river that drained into,the wide inlet from the mountain range close by.cortez told them the river is 60 feet deep for 5 miles,then is more shallow as it rises to its mountain spring source.all the men were standing around the chart on the captains table,and thinking fast about the best tactics and strategy ot adopt.cortez rolled out,another map to mark there exact position,and ordered sancho to use a sextant to obtain a accurate sighting.the lattitude and longtitude were marked on the chart.captain boone did his own,sighting to verify the position.cortez said,there is a sharp bend in the river,half way along its length.we can winch the vessel to the shore,and mount 30 carronades on the hill above the vessel.we have lots of chinese rockets left,and can set up a barrage on any ship venturing up the trujillo river. A fire aboard spells death to any ship and the crew.captain jones said,get chavez koonah and sancho to get all the weapons we need ashore,and in position.cortez and sancho returned by boat to the jackal. The three remaining captians discussed plans in detail.i will meet you in jamiaca in a months timeas,we have much to discuss about our future,and your return voyage to france.captain james boone,was rowed back to his ship and he went aboard,thinking about the letter in his pocket.captian jones told him of vandetta and cormorant sailing ahead on patrol,and to keep a lookout for them.so it turned out to be,that conatact was made,just before dusk two days later. three vessels were to the south,a huge 74 gun battleship and two smaller ships.a barqua and a frigate anchored a 100 feet apart.as oslo sailed towards them,captian boone noticed the two smaller vessels flew yankee flags a cutter headed for oslo,as soon as the ship hove too.de villier and big koonah came aboard on the rope ladder,let down for them by the crew.its a pleasure to meet you sir,let us retire to my cabin.i have some excellent jamaican rum,made by my distillery. I sailed to ireland last year,to find a good manager.semus devlin is his name,i tripled his wage,and shipped his whole family out to jamaica.we make brandy,rum and gin at shannon brewery,named after my great granpa who blew himself to hell,with a home made still.de villier,laughed heartliy and took a sip of rum.he licked his lips and took another large mouthful,and said mmm yes very good indeed,not your average rotgut rubbish one is served in london taverns or on the docks.now down to bussiness boone,after i sailed south from ecuador i came upon the plymouth,the 74 gun vessel you obsereved. it was 3 hours after sunset when i saw 5 peruvain pirate vessels grapple onto the the ship.the british battle ship opened fire,but could not depress the guns low enough to any target.some pirates got aboard and were shot by marines.comorant attacked and destroyed 3 pirate vessels,with her 18 pounder guns.the other pirtate ships tried to set fire to the plymouth,and vandetta sailed to her stern and used hot cannon shot to set the pirate boats on fire.listen carefully james,the name of the british captain is henry dobson,my alias name is captain benjamin franklin and my home port is san diego.comorants captian is marcel dupont,a half english and half french.he is fluent in french understood captian boone.yes thank you for a full explaination,now please read the letter from my dear first cousin captian smthye jones.de villier sipped wine as he read the four page letter,then he put the letter in his wallet.captain dobson has invited us to dine aboard,no doubt he will be interested to meet the norwegian captian of the oslo.he said. I have papers de villier,a mere nothing old chap.captain lars olsen master mariner at your service,we shall take a dozen botlles of my finest with us when we board the plymouth.captain henry dobson was under a shade cloth on deck painting a seascape,with 2 middy.s at hand with piant and brushes .,when the two captains came aboard.please sit and relax gents,and have some cheese and biscut,and earl grey. A few final touches and my work,shall be finsihed.dinner will be served in 3 hours by my italian chef antonio,a master at kitchen endeavours what.four crew from oslo placed 2 casks and several boxes in the captians cabin.de villier sent a crew to vandetta,to get six paintings he had found on one of the spanish galleons.they returned and put them in the captains cabin.mario the italian chef came on deck,and shouted,de master piece is a served admirale,you must eat now,before de dish a grows a cold si,and walked back inside.quickly gents into my cabin,or mario will start waving that meat cleaver of his. dinner and drinks were served. A soup,seafood and pasta dishes.captian boone said,de villier has some stolen spanish paintings for you to study,and sir you may care to taste my own brand of gin rum and brandy.then put 3 bottles on the table.by all means,steward bring 3 fresh glasses to sample his wares by gad.his vessel oslo a barque is ten knots faster,than my frigate henry a very well designed ship,with the best of timbers used by french shipwrights.an old viking ship design form norway. Dobson took a mouthful of shannan brandy,swirled it around his mouth,and swallowed it slowly.then he made a few notes,on a parchment next to his glass.after tasting the rum and gin,he called for jameson the chief puser.jameson arrived at the rush,and they had a whispered conversation.captain hobson then wrote out an order for 50 casks of rum,10 of gin and 30 casks of special issue brandy. the war with china was discussed at dinner,and hobson mentioned the transfer of many warships from normal duties around the coast of england. what interested de villier most.was admiralty orders to remove all the patrol vessels in the english channel,leaving only small sloop.s of the customs service.de villier made notes as they chatted,and learnt more about admiral rhodes and the china squadron.semus devlin will deliver you goods to you,in jamaica sir,i bid you good evening .thank you for a fine dinner and extend my compliments to mario,the chef.200 leagues north of vandetta,captain jones was under a large sail cloth on deck.he had a glass of french brandy at hand,and tins of oils and wax.across his lap was saladin,s sword,the original stolen from windsor castle. A group of young middy.s were admiring a gold replica laying in red velvet,in a cedar box.middies tolly and johnson asked how much yon sword be worth,captian jones said it was worth the same as all the jewels in the tower of london.tolly said poppycock it be only one sword,and there is huge diamond form africa worth 10000 swords.johnson said aye and lots more rubies an emeralds in the tower place.ooh my goodness you caught me out lads,now diago get some food for your young friends,and more brandy for me.i have a good story to tell you all.now a great arab bedoiun warrior salah ad din yussef ibn ayyub,which is his true kurdish name,he was born at tikrit,on the river tigris and grew to be an intelligent man,his natural ability on horse and with the sword was noticed by selyuk. A noble statesmen and very experienced soldier.he sent him to military college,to be trained for war.after that he went to egypt,to fight against the crusaders from england and europe.do you remeber richard the loin heart lads,from the histroy lessons i gave you.si capitano

Chapter 4

t his salah adin he was a generale in the army yes.said diago.no he was a sultan and he beat king richard in a huge battle.yes you are right johnson at fyord of jacobs daughter in1179 he wiped out all the crusader knights and won in allepo.that is enough for now as i have to oil and sharpen the sword on a stone.later more stories will be told,now back to your duties if you please.the jackal was cruising at 26 knots out at sea,on her patrol run seeking the french frigates. swordfish and alverez lay at anchor in pisco bay. food and water was bought from the natives,and they gave them axes knives powder,shot and good english rifles.the crews of both vessels killed much game animals to feed the local natives,and the ships doctors went ashore to tend to the sick.the agreed stragey was to let the two french frigates enter the bay,then the jackal would enter behind them.the three pirate ships were to catch them in a viciuos crossfire from 3 ships at once.at precisely noon,as cortez had predicted in his message sent by spotty,a big fat pigeon sancho had let go from jackal,the two french frigates entered pisco bay.the first frigate cruised back and forth,across the entrance,while the second frigate sailed slowly around the bay.the officers aboard were checking each,river entrance and the shoreline intently.the two frigates sailed to meet and anchored beside each other.a french boat was rowed up into each river for only a short distance,and both ships returned at a cannon siganl.just then the jackal entered the bay,with a cuban flag and sailed past the french frigate to heave to,along side swordfish.a boat with 6 officers and crew left the frigate nantes and was rowed to swordfish,captain fecamp came aboard with 5 senior officers,he said to captain jones i am under orders from the spanish government to inspect all vessels along this coast.present your shpis papers now captain.captian jones was holding a long barreled english rifle on his lap sitting in a deck chairand said.listen carefully i shall only say this once,we are a dutch trading fleet of ships and spain and france have no juristiction at law of the sea,over my vessels. what are these dutch vessels doing here. where do you sail from. I intend searching them both for stolen contraband or traces of spanish treasure said fecamp.sa you like fecamp and do no damage or you will fed to the sharks mon ami said jones.when fecamp left to search the swordfish capt.jones whispered orders to the 3 middies to follow the frenchmen,at all times and report later. he poured 3 small glasses for the boys,who returned within an hour .the french officers had gone.have a wee dram of rum lads,johnson your observations first please,of what the french ahve done since boarding our ship.johnson said the big toad face fecamp.looked in each hold careful like.then he picks up a bit of oak wood ta carpenter left behind and strange it were to see him tappin there low down and up high on the bulkheads,he had his men all doin the same too sir.thank you middy.

tolly .diago any more to add.yes sir me eagle eyes saw that skinny marine sargeant,he had a bent with him.he tried to push it behind the wood,but bosun connolly moved in close,and wagged that big arab dagger of in yon frenchies face.get off this ship ya dirty craupard he yells real loud.percy and dobsie had crossbows aimed at the skinny runt.got scared and letf they did.siad tolly excellent tolly.there are 25 secret comaprtments,gents in the number 1 hold and you need a special key to open them.a spring lock releases a latch,and must be truned the right way.after a search of the sloop,the french cutter returned to the frigate nantees .both vessles set sail and left the bay of pisco.alvarez the sloop followed the french ships at a distance .the galleon was sailed out,into the bay and swordfish and jackal escorted her out of pisco bay .the sloop returned 3 days later and all 4 ships headed for dead man.s cove,on the island of jamaica.cortez noticed the old,jetty had beed repaired with new timbers,and 50 wagons were drawn up. A blue lamp signal was made by sancho and they heard a group of pirates come down the jetty.with a red answering signal lamp.

the mississipi was unloaded and the loot,taken to the refinery at wilkonson sword factory.a rest of two weeks for the crews,and the ships would be repaired and careened.now the goldsmith would start work,and capt jones rode into town to see him.he gave torez a case of rum and saldin,s sword and the small gold replica made in england by the duke de montrief.the horse engaved on the hilt senor is simoon, meaning desert wind,the favourite horse of the sultan a black andalusion stallion.my grand father was ambassador to egypt and brought many books home about the sultan,s history.torez said .the two men went inside for a hot spicy spanish dinner cooked by the goldsmith,s wife jacinta. after 6 months senor torez had completed his task of creating 3 gold replica.s of saladin,s sword and 3 treasures from10tons of lead ballast. which had been gold plated.small and large ingots indentical to those,made by the spanish mint in madrid.all the jewels had the stones taken out,and gold melted down.the stones would be sold later. genuine gold bars would be used,as samples to sell each treasure,now in sturdy wooden boxes which had all been padlocked for saftey.the four ships,swordfish,vandetta jackal and mississpi loaded all the loot,and sailed for england,and dover the dukes residence on the coast.just a day before they left,a mail boat calypso arrived with a letter for captain de villier.the 3 new clippers he ordered had been completed.loaded with supplies and were ready to sail,at the good captain,s leisure.at 11 of the clock,off dover the lookout shouted, blue lampthorne off the port bow sir.it be on the mast of a ship,and comin quick like.a sleek racing yacht came alongside vandetta and captian hanson yelled out a message through his megaphone.follow my stern exactly,do not veer of course there are hidden reefs on both sides of the channel de villier. the two pirate ships,followed the yacht in line astern,and moored at the long jetty at he dukes mansion.two months later the mississpi and the sloop alverez,arrived,after selling there cargo of gold in america.the cormorant and barracuda were already,at anchor at dover castle and had been unloaded of all cargo.the crews rested for 2 weeks,then small crews sailed vandetta swordfish,and barracuda to to the new buyers in holland.the jackal sailed to spain.to unload a fake treasure,for don miguel de sante,a corrupt treasurry official the don had 50 soldiers dressed as peasants,so his actions would not alert any local officials,of his secret dealings.cortez then sailed to holland to.pick up the crews of the pirate ship and returned to dover.the

Chapter 5

duke de montfreit, had arranged the sale of the the 3 pirate ships through lloyds of london shipping agents of which he owned a 40% interest.captians jones and de villier delivered the second,fake treasure and sword to le harve at midnight on the french coast in the vessel stern plate name trumped in french to suit the occasion,alias the jackal.30 large horse drawn wagons came along side to unload the cargo. the boxes of gold were marked as gunpowder for the french army.de villier gave general la fayette a cedar box with a saladin gold sword in the captians cabin,and de villier showed him real gold bar samples.the trumped vessel set sail,as soon as it was unloaded,and set a course for marseille,on the east coast of france.late at night 25 scruffy looking seaman came on board.capt smythe jones .hugged a huge man,over 6 feet tall with a scar on his left cheek.gents may i present my old first leftanent now semi retired marcel pacino a tour guide,so i hear.all present laughed at this wild inaccurate statement. marcel was the leader of the french underworld,and his men were loading 200 kegs of stolen french cognac at the present moment.the men enjoyed a four course meal,and got down to business.smythe jones showed marcel a list of cargo aboard,who read it and smiled.the weapons i need now,as that swine charles monet is trying to wipe out my whole smuggling operation on the east coast.said marcel. does he have any brothers marcel said smythe jones. but of course,cardinal is his older brother,i know the scum well and all about his corrupt methods. he has a liking for young boys.my sister,s daughter is a maid,in the house across the road from his chateau in paris said marcel.excellent marcel,now we have also brought you 3 arab stallions,and 2 mares for breeding.one horse each for you and your two sons.they were bought from the spanish riding school at barcelona,by captain cortez.the colonel in charge tried to report manual cortez his father to the inquisition authorities.his body was never found,and worked for ultima the catholic church spy network.cardinal monet is to be proven corrupt,so we need all his papers as evidence to expose his illegal actions to the vatican in rome. later i want you to make,sure he suffer.s a long and painful death.said smythe jones.there is a large pig farm i own along the coast,we use to dispose of our enemy,s. I just hope the pigs do not choke,on the fat cardinal,s carcase,mon capitane.they all had a good laugh,and de villier gave marcel a long ebony wood box.inside the box was a german mauser sniper.s rifle with along telescopic sight mounted on top. two six shot smith and weston,revolvers and a set of 12 daggers .a present for saving my life,marcel when that french captian tried to run me through with his rapier at toulon.a knock at the door was heard and de vliier said enter.bosun connolly who said all cargo loaded,we be ready to sail,sir.marcel picked up his box said goodbye and left the ship. we must do a spot of business first bosun and 6 days later,were seated at a table in marcels house. on a large table,were several parchments with the embossed vatican crest of state,many papers, a gold signet ring and the robes of a cardinal. 3 chests of different sizes,lay on the floor.a small wizened grey haired man, picked up each chest,and with a set of lock picks opended each one .then he put them on the table.the first was full of daimond,sand rubies. the second held gold cions of many kinds.the third and biggest chest contained 3 large tomes,like a captains log book.cortez opened the first book,and saw a list of family names and members,on each page.the date of death and an amountin francs written.then two more words heretic,inquisition. cortez found 3 of his family were tortured to death. de villier checking the second book,found a list of all persons killed,the a list of cash and gold under 3 cardinals names.two spanish and one french,which was monet .smythe jones read the third book which,had a list of wills,values of estates,monies kept in banks and the totals beside each name.in all the value was 362,420 gold dubloons.he had a sip of madeira,and said,gents i believe we have more than enough evidence to expose all 3 cardinals,and we shall have copies made.we keep the original documents as i do not trust those devious swine in the vatican.the three men went through all the rest of the papers,and agreed ona good plan. francis o leary,a small chubby,smiling priest with glasses was given a large goblet of brandy,and he had four plates of canapes cheese,ham and hot stew bedise him.father o leary we have a secret mission for you,to take a parcel of letters to the senior cardinal in paris.you will have 4 body guards with you,at all times so need not be concerned with your saftey understood father,de villier said.he handed the priest the third book to read,and went shopping for more cuban cigars.3 hrs later de villier returned and asked the priest if he would carry out the mission,to which he agreed.now we shall bring you back aboard my vessel,after you have completed your task.you will be given new identity papers,as the owner of a farm in england.in this leather bag is 10000 pounds in gold coins for you, i advise you,never to return to france or go back to ireland.leave the church forever as you are 21 years of age and have a full life ahead of you. There are several of my seaman who live near you,on the farm,they will protect you.father o leary got on a coach with four seaman and,off they went to paris. Captians jones and de villier were sipping ale,under sunshades when marcel and captain montoya came aboard at midday.more ale and two chairs arrived for the guests.marcel handed a roll of parchments tied with a red silk ribbon,who unrolled them on the table before him.the first was from cardinal rizzoni,asking for complete and utter confidentialty. from the three captains about the papers sent to the vatican.in return he would let them know,what action the vatican did in future.the second letter from the popes secretary said all docements had proven tobe false,and cardinal monet was totally innocent of all charges.de villier collected the parchments and said marcel,a wagon load to the pig farm is required sir.one month later,there were 15 murders on the west coast of france.7 more murders and apparent accidents occured in paris. three staff from the ministry off the interior,two senior police officers and two pawnbrokers.the jackal sailed for barcelona,to pick up four men with special talents and ability .safe cracker,s and burglars,all recent crew men of barraccuda. then jackal sailed to dover.in the stately lounge,of the duke de montfreit castle.with all present,the duke rang a small bell and stood up.to say.i have irrefutable evidence affidavids and 65

Chapter 6

ittnesses of the ten men,who have caused us all so much pain and trouble in the past. I have had consultatios,with 3 dukes and 2 barons,and of course several barristers at law.we will present our case at the old bailey this month gentleman.six men were hanged,the other four sentenced to life trems in prison.more legal actions in france and spain and all lands and money.s returned to the four men.120men in three counties governments were jailed for numerous crimes each year three finely made clipper.s arrive at dover,on april fools day for the la trumped feast and celebration.on each of the tables layed out is a finely carved pirate,made of soft huon pine.it was

painted by a master monsieur renoir in france.in the small pirates right hand is a gold arab sword,with a ivory handle. An engraved name plate is fixed to the bottom of the carving base.two names are seen in arabic and english SALAH AD DIN YUSSIF IBN AYYUB and in english SALADIN. On the night of the 12th celebration at dover castle,de villier produced a music box,on the lid was painted 3 ships,each had a flag flowing in the sea wind on the topmast with the name of each ship.underneath flew 3 jolly rogers and in the top left hand corner were 3 bags of gold dubloons.in the top right hand corner was a princess in a blue ball gown wearing a diamond tiara. De villier opened the music box,and all the men present listened andsang along to an old sea shanty blow boys blow,about the yankee clipper history at sea. .ps it is estimated there is $12 billion in spanish treasure on the bottom of the sea.6,30PM TEUSDAY APRIL 28TH 2015 THE END

The Secret of
the Scrimshaw

midshipman willy dykes aged twenty was sitting at a table in the eight bells Tavern,with Toby Benson the Bosun .A huge man at six foot two and broad shouldered,from Yorkshire .with them was Binty Scrimmins the tough little cockney from Soho, in the east end of London. He was the sailing master of the merchant vessel Grenoble, with thirty two guns and weighed six hundred tons.They were all tucking into some smoked trout,with hot vegetables and thick slabs of buttered bread.The conversation around the table was about the carving art of scrim shaw,Toby and Binty had amassed a huge collection bones each, most of the them handed down through three generations of there families. Willy was dead keen to learn to carve and had three sea chests full whales teeth.He even had four small elephant tusks as well.Binty said,me be two score old now,and Monty me grandpa taught me ta bone carve like, from when I was a young nipper.He was a Master Builder at the time,loved to carve soap, wood, clay anything handy Willy. Well my dad and grand pappy were both sea

Officers,they was in whaling clippers .Both of them been a carving since first watch on board. Toby said. We leave for Kingston in four days time Captain Bunn told me so we will have lots of spare time to do scrim shaw when we is not on duty.said Willy Binty said, what cargo do we have for the Caribee, loads of luxuries for the Governor I suppose,and fancy dresses and stuff for all the ladies like scent or fume smelling bottles.Well now keep this to yourselves right, Its secret between us.We be loading boxes marked herbs and spices that weigh three ton, which is really gold bullion. to pay the navy and all the workers Barklay,s Bank wll collect it with a big escort from the navy. To do business wth the towns folk and plantation owners see. Willy whispered. Toby said Bloody hell, I Hope no one about the Plymouth dockyards finds out,word would spread like wild fire.Lots of them privateers between England and the Bahamas no doubt about that me bucko. Binty said,too right Binty me old mate, only been in two scraps .Once with them oily looking rag heads in Zanzibar and in India.Arabs they was in three dhows.them arabs tried to sneak up on our ship at night but we all was lying doggo below the deck rail until the last minute.Copped a wopping great broadside from port and starboard guns the ragheads did,blew them to hell and only two survivor,s matey. Toby said .Willy said mum.s the word then, now Binty can you be showing me how to carve on my elephant tusk,and use the blue ink to give my piece a bit of colour.I have my father,s tool kit which I cleaned,oiled the leather bag to soften it you know .Toby and me will show you the carving tricks and how to sharpen all the knives and different shaped tools.We best be getting some extra like more inks and an oil stone for you,before we goes back aboard the Grenoble.They chatted on for two more hours about the coming voyage and what they needed to buy tomorrow, then retired to a warm bed in the Tavern.On a warm sunny morning the Grenoble set sail for Gibralter,to stay for a week then on to the port of Valletta in Malta. The water they took aboard at this time was tainted and made the crew sick.Delaying them for more than a month.Willy and his mates were okay as they had worked ashore and not drunk any water aboard ship.when all was well again, the ship sailed to Malta.The trade goods were off loaded and Grenoble set off for Antigua island to deliver trade goods to plantation owner, s. The crew had sighted several ships along the way usually in a convoy of three vessels for safety. Some were navy mail packets,those heaved too and sent a small boat over with mail and the latest news from Plymouth. From London semaphores passed fast messages from one high hill to another, with a signal system to the coastal cities such as Plymouth.then the information was written down and passed to ships at sea .Return mail was sent to friends and family. As the ship sailed west willy learned most of there was to know, about the art of carving from his two good mates late into the night,when all three men were off duty.Wood scraps from the carpenters little workshop were used first,soap, ivory bits and pieces. Later wooden arms and legs were made for injured seaman who had lost a limb in battle,or whose luck turned with a bad accident on board .A small puppet set was made which provided fun and entertainment for the crew, Barney Rubble the ships doctor was most pleased as it was good for the crews morale.Three quarters of the way across the Atlantic ocean, the lookout in the crows nest shouted, sail ho on the port bow.Captain Bunn used his glass to check the ship and said, A yanky by the look of the flag,he was an ex royal navy captain and became alert immediatley .The crew of the other ship were wearing loose Spanish shirts and trousers, not the tough blue serge coats the yankee,s liked best at sea .He said to Harrison the first leiutenant load and roll out all guns quietly Harrison, marksman into the rigging.double shot in the stern and bow guns,The crew to stay out of sight below the deck rail,lie low you understand surprise is half the battle won,before it even starts. The crew on the yanky ship waved in a friendly manner as it closed on the merchant ship.The captain of the other ship and three of his crew, all had telescopes on Grenoble when they sailed past. Oregon was her name which captain Bunn now saw,a schooner of twenty guns eighteen pound size he guessed.Most of the crew had black or dark brown skin which verified his doubts about a false flag on the yanky vessel.He ordered the helmsman to steer to port and asked for more sails aloft to out sail the Oregon. As time went by he knew the other vessel was lighter in the water thereby faster .Also better and larger sails that looked new,very white and strong full in the wind.Toby was with his two cobber,s on the starboard guns,was pestering willy who was watching Oregon and every move she made through his glass. What is happening be jesus, them is bloody pirates from some island here about, for sure willy said Toby. Flaming oath look at the sloppy sails and ropes hanging all over the place, not like the yanks I have seen.said Binty. Captain Bunn, ordered the top sails taken in to reduce speed then turned his ship about to come up along side Oregon.He saw then a French flag flying from her top most masthead.Harrison sight the guns and fire at will,on the roll,he said. He ordered a broadside from the starboard guns as they passed, telling the gunners to aim for each of the masts.A withering blast followed, then he came about again and used his port side guns to rake the stern of Oregon.After he passed the other ship, he fired his four rear twenty four pound guns into the stern and scored a direct hit. On the quarter deck of Oregon the blast killed six men and injured ten more .The battle between the two ships raged on for two more hours, then Billy Menton gunners mate shot the top off the Oregon,s main mast. It came tumbling down with sails and rigging and the Oregon lost way. Grenoble sailed in closer and used hot shot cannon balls to set the other ship alight, This port broadside hit all along the Oregon and it caught fire in three places.The crew of the Oregon fought the fire to no avail, knowing there ship as lost they took to the small boats they had aboard as the fire increased along the length of the vessel.After lowering the boats or loading with loot and supplies of food and water, the crews rowed like hell in fear of being burnt alive.willy ordered the gunner near him to sink the small pirate boats which they did in short order.The merchant ship set a new course for Jamaica. Two leagues from the Virgin Islands in the Carribee, huge black storm clouds gathered coming in fast from the west.The wind picked up to gale force and heavy rain slammed down on the ship. All hands were ordered to take in all sail, only leaving the fore sail and jib sail for steerage way from the helm.The wind blew much stronger and forced the ship off course.it was pitch black,and no man aboard knew, the ship was sailing towards a wide sharp dangerous reef .Beyond lay Pinosa Island inhabited only by local natives. All of a sudden a loud tearing crunch came from the bow,the ship shuddered and leaned to port. Gale force winds increased the danger to the crew,by smashing the ships hull again and again, viciously against the long jagged reef. The ship was now holed in the places and taking in water fast the captain ordered all boats over the side.Then loaded them with food and fresh water plus of course there dunnage.Captain Bunn asked Harrison his second in command to inspect below deck with Chips Thomas the carpenter,to see if the ship could be saved.He set off at a rush to secure all the ships papers logs and valuable navigation sextant.The barometer he took off its hook on the wall,bundled up his sword and a large bag of books. Dragging his chest behind him he made for the boats shouting for assistance with his gear.Tie all the cutters and jolly boats together now so we don,t loose each other in the storm,said the captain. As the boats rowed away the Grenoble was slammed by huge waves which forced the length of the hull against the sharp reef.The masts went first torn to shreds as they broke into pieces when the the vessel collapsed on its side. Cannons and cargo were scattered all over the reef,or floated away in all directions.The little fleet of boats rowed along the length of the reef looking for a channel through the reef,until Captain Bunn ordered a long rest .Dawn is the best time to carry on as we can see nothing in this infernal storm at night he said.The crews dropped anchors and settled down to sleep where they could in the darkness.A lighter blue on the horizon to the east gave notice dawn would soon appear.The captain saw this and said nothing.The men needed a good sleep he thought,so let them be he ordered those officers who were still awake.At noon Bosun Toby Benson roused the crews from there slumber,up and away me bucko,s he shouted.

There was lots of grumbles and groans from the men and many insults shouted at Toby,then the fleet got under way.Within a short time a small gap was noticed in the reef by Samuel Finn a fore top man,who threw a lead out to check the depth.The first cutter edged into the channel and Samuel shouted six fathoms captain, plenty of room ship mates.It was only after the first boat came easily through the channel, did the crew see an island with eight hundred natives,spread along the shore. Well bugger me land tucker and native gals suits me fine said Chips No bloody heavin deck we be able to rest the old bones shipmate said Toby. Several native out rigger canoes came out to meet the small fleet of British boats,waving and smiling they made a circle around them and rowed very fast for shore.Captain Bunn ordered the crews to follow he had some doubt,s as the natives looked very fierce with bones through there ears and noses .Also feathers were stuck out from the wild bush hair they had sticking out every where.When the british sailors arrived on shore the hoard of natives came down to help them unload the boats .Then all the boats were dragged above the high tide line and the sailors were led to big warm fires to dry off.A good hot meal put the men in good cheer and they made off for the huts the Cheif Bowanga had given them.The very tired men slept for a good many hours until late the next day and were woken by young native boys and girls bringing fresh fruit and coconut milk for breakfast. Harrison the first lieutenant had three junior midshipmen make a head count of all present, to find out who was missing after the disaster of the ship wreck.Willy with two native boys Momba and Owenga his new friends, wandered around chatting to the injured men and Dr Barney Rubble.The lack of a good supply of medicine and bandages was of serious concern, so Owenga on hearing about this suggested he see Ngoomo the Medicine man and Shaman. Both men came back later with two big strong native girls carrying large pots on there heads. These were full of herbs and healing lotions to wrap around injured arms and legs. The girls were the daughters of the chief .Within a month most of the men had healed well with the care of six medical people to attend them. Willy wondered where old Binty was,no one had seen him since a big wave had washed him overboard from there cutter on the night of the storm.Three officers and a full crew of twenty men sailed a cutter out to the wreck, where sixty seven dead bodies were all over the boat and on top of the reef,most had been savaged by sharks crabs and the like.The men sought any worth while cargo left and found many a floating chest and barrel which they loaded aboard and headed for shore.Harrison informed the captain sir he said we have two hundred and fifteen crew on this island sixty seven dead at the wreck,so that leaves eighteen missing at my count,Very good work lad said Captain Bunn we shall salvage much from the wreck, then later i will send a search party out for a week with a definite plan.Aye aye sir and i would say there is one hundred tons of cargo on or near the reef,Harrison said. With a combined workforce of five hundred men and women, sailing lots of boats of all sizes only a matter of weeks was taken before all the worth while cargo had been brought ashore.Chips Thomas the carpenter asked willy and his two native mates to help him to check, and mark any good wood left on the wreck. Large gangs of men would strip this lot out, working in watches as they normally did when aboard the ship at sea. At a third of the wood could be used.spare undamaged masts,sail material and many other items.The natives and crew dived down to secure ropes to small cannons, to be hauled out and any item trapped in the hull.Fifty of the crew rowed out in boats once a week to collect floatsum along the length of the reef .The natives showed them how to lash two out riggers together to load food,barrels of gun powder,weapons and small sakers.There was very ships passing the remote island pinosa,one of the many virgin islands. Toby and Willy dived down into there cabins and found the boxes of ivory and bones.Willy was lucky on his third dive,when he managed to drag the chest of carving tools out from his cabin One Afternoon a week later, willy opened a wooden box from the Grenoble and smiled good he thought the maps are wrapped in oilskins.They were in good condition when he unwrapped them and were the charts used to train the midshipmen in navigation. Toby, Willy and Charles Essex the youngest of the midshipman aboard Grenoble,built a large wooden shed with timber from the wreck.Then set about building up a good huge supply of food of all kinds near there cave on the highest hill on the island .They cleaned all the carving tools and collected bones from the natives and along the shore of the island .The medicine man Nogoomo,helped the ships doctor heal the injured men of the crew,but sadly three men died.There wounds had turned septic and gangrene set in .There was eight hundred natives on the island,with plenty of wild game,fruit and vegetables.Captain bunn made certain all the crew,ate lots of limes and lemons with a variety of fruits to prevent scurvy in the men.The senior officers sat around the camp fire one night to discuss the future.many suggestions were put forward and argued over in deatail.The captain asked Chips the carpenter if he could build a thirty foot boat, to sail to the nearest large port to get help from the local governor.From maps retrieved from the wreck and sightings taken on the island the senior officers had worked out there location.To sail in any direction from pinosa island,without the local knowledge of reefs, shoals and many other dangers could prove fatal.The carpenter replied a boat can be built,but with no proper caulking and a copper lined hull, the boat will not last long in the open sea.Two weeks later nogoomo the medicine man came to to the carpenters hut four wrapped bundles of palm leaves.chips he said this is for your boat .A Tree sap and juice from the palm tree,this stops the water from coming in your boat.keep them wet all the time until you use it .This proved to be the case when the carpenter built his boat.he took the fininshed vessel out three times to check for any leaks .The captain ordered the boat to be made,with all hands to help the carpenter.In two months the thirty foot cutter was finished,with a carved name plate.master craftsman,h. m. s.chipps .I t had two masts and a simple lanteen sail found on arab dhows.Then a long discussions started with the natives, about there local knowledge of the sea,other islands nearby.Every thing they knew in fact, was vital if a crew were to survive a voyage.

Did many ships pass the islands,if so when and how many.Willy had made good friends with two big native boys his own age,Momba and Owenga and one day they rowed out to the wreck in a native canoe .The natives were good divers and could go much deeper than the white men.Owenga came up from a dive with a small leather bag.Smiling he handed the bag to Willy who undid the string holding the bag together. When Willy opened the bag he saw a lot of mud and salt inside.He dipped his hand in and pulled out three silver coins,and he gave one each to his native friends .Again he delved into the bag and found two large gold sovereigns,and slipped them in his pocket quickly so no one would see them.With sign language and sketches he made with chalk,he got Owenga to show him exactly where he found the bag.He marked the details down with quill and ink in his log book .H told the two native boys to say nothing to anyone,a secret to which they agreed.Willy let Charles and Toby know of his find thay day,and they celebrated for three days by getting drunk down along the shore away from the main camp .Toby told the officers they needed more bones,sea shells and drift wood for there fires and for carving.When the came back from there trip Willy decided to make a map of the whole island,and the location of the gold bullion near the wreck,so he could find it later.James heron a leftanant had informed him the gold bullion was worth four hundred thousand pounds.As it was insured by Lloyds of London,it would be unlikely anyone would come to salvage anything from the wreck at all.Willy on a mere midshipman,s wages of six florins a month,only had a vague idea of just how great a fortune that was .Toby,Willy and the two native boys went diving again on the wreck until they had one hundred coins in total.They decided that was enough and brought them ashore in rotten barrels of meat,claiming the needed the wood to make a small boat. Toby Willy and Charles made lots of useful tools and many chairs,tables and sets of shelves for the native women.Long benches for the elder natives to sit on in the shade,three legged stools and beds .Hooks were made for fishing and long sturdy fishing poles.Washing tubs for the girls and large framed fans,controlled with ropes,to keep the natives cool in summer.The Captain decided it was time to sail for help,and with two natives as guides a twenty men crew and two officers set sail for Puerto Rico.There were many islands of the natives ran or were helped to cover,in along there course,where they could get food and fresh water,and with luck and good seamanship they would make it.At dawn a week later,huge dark storm clouds formed and a large water tornado formed sucking all the sea into the sky .This tornado passed to the north of Pinosa island,and the winds increased to gale force.Willy and his friends were in there cave with Owenga and Momba,cooking the days catch of fish and crabs.Owenga said,with pictures he drew in the sand,all the natives go to the hills and caves when the big storms come.The birds and waves tell them and the big winds get angry,so they go quickly to safety.Willy had buried his loot at the back of the cave,a much better place than a native hut in the native village.The ferocious winds hit the island,ripping away everything in its path,most of the natives went to caves or got beneath there huts.The British crew stayed in there huts,and some even took to small boats to sail into small inlets for safety.The storm passed the island and then a hurricane come swirling in from the east with gale force winds .Willy was in the cave with all his friends cooking fish and crabs they had caught fresh that day.Toby raced out to put any things lying around in the hut,then locked the doors and windows .He had a good look around with his telescope and went running back to the cave .He said bloody real bad matey,s never seen the like a killerhurricane for sure .After four long hours of wild ferocious winds the winds calmed and screaming and yelling could be heard from the injured .Thirty six natives died and two hundred and ten british crew men,and thirty more died later from bad injuries .Fifteen white men were left.as the doctor and all the officers were battered to death or drowned .willy was now the senior officer of fourteen men as a midshipman.Three big native outriggers came from londo island just twenty miles from pinosa island.These natives were of the same tribe and inter related by marriage.There was a small feast after the dead were buried and the londo natives stayed for three months then sailed back home.Many weeks passed during which news came that wreckage had been found of there sloop,and three half eaten dead bodies by sharks. So no word had been passed to any one at Puerto Rico,thus no ship would come to there rescue.Only two boats from Grenoble were left,a twenty foot cutter and a six foot jolly boat.Ten of the men left on Pinosa wanted to try and sail to Kingston,Willy disagreed but Toby said best to let the men go as they were very good sailors.To force them to stay may cause bloodshed he warned Willy .All the men helped load the vessel and launch it into the breakers .THey waved to Willy as the cutter went through the entrance channel in the reef.The cutter headed south east finding small islands along the way and stopping to fish and get water for there barrels.In a months time they sighted the large island of Antigua.As luck would have it,there landing place was on the north side of the island. After eating and drinking with the local natives,there cheif mandoona told them very bad pirates live in the south, with big fire ships go bang bang and waved his arms around.Four ships all captured frigates it was learnt were at anchor in a large bay. There were rumours of Hawkins, Black beard and even the terror of the seas Captain mad dog Morgan himself.No one really knew and were too scared to ask,for fear of getting there throat slit wide open. The ten british crew men sneaked along the shore through the mangroves for a much closer inspection of the bay. Right at the tip of the headland a Barracoon vessel was anchored flying a yankee flag. The pirates knew well never to harm any yankee sailors as there was fifty yankee ships sailing all around the carribean all year round.The british men took a wide course around the island and tied up there cutter next to the yankee ship.Then one man went aboard to visit the captain of the vessel Redfin.Captain Santos was his name,and he had just lost seven of his crew who had gone to join the pirates.The cruel sadistic swine in charge of the was an ex convict wanted for sixteen murders of british women and children at a missionary on puerto rico.Miguel Riouse was the dogs name,a filhty low animal a hyena of the sea.He never took any prisoners at sea or on land,instead his men would cut or slashed there bodies to draw fresh blood. Over the side they went as shark bait while he laughed and drank the best french cognac from a bottle.His three brothers were the captains of the other pirate ships .Simon Donald was seated with Captain Santos in his cabin sipping a glass of bourbon .What is your name lad and how may i be of help,have a slug of that fine kentucky bourbon. You look tired and worn out said captain Santos .Simon said we be ten crew from a British merchant ship Grenoble out of Portsmouth your honour.A big storm hit us hard and smashed the poor old girl on a reef .Simon O,Donald be me name sir .Where did the ship hit the reef,I know these waters well,and how many are alive now said captain Santos.There is only four men and Willy the young midshipman left on Pinosa island,the rest were killed in a hurricane about two hundred at a guess said Simon.Pinosa is due north from this vessel,s position on my map and Grenoble was on her voyage to San Domingo and Kingston with a cargo of trade goods is that correct Simon said the Captain.Yes that is the course many ships take in the carribee.said Simon .Well we must report the loss of the Grenoble to the Governor in Jamaica and the big sloop that left our island got wrecked in the storm.All twenty five hands dead in that bloody storm.You care to sign on as crew with me son tell your mates there welcome also.Then go to the galley cooky will give you some good food. Twenty of my crew joined forces with the pirates,the fools they will not live long,mark my words .They both stood up and shook hands to seal the deal,later all ten english men would sign the crew ledger. Simon went out of the cabin first to tell his mates the news of a new berth aboard Redfin.Then the captain led them around the Louisiana made ship. It was a very well crafted vessel and had just been careened and fully repainted .Captain Santos had the crew unload and winch the cutter aboard,then the carpenter William Trent repaired and gave it three new coats of paint .The english men met the rest of the crew who were mostly negro and a few white men.All these men were mostly from different places in the gulf of mexico .They were fed and given new clothes large bush hats and wet weather gear.Danny watson aged twenty had been due to sit for his middy exam on board Grenoble,and went to the captain to discuss the matter. The captain heard him out and said its alright lad,you stay by me on the day watch and i shall teach you the ropes okay.Thankee captain i will do my best Danny said .later that night the captain sent big Jimbo a happy huge smiling negro with a message for Simon .Jimbo found him sitting on a barrel by the main mast,whittling a piece of wood into the shape of a dolphin.You be simon,capn tol me ta give ya this and handed him an envelope. Simon laughed as Jimbo had an english cockney accent and gave Jimbo a mug of rum.The message read. In one weeks time we are to leave port for Puerto Rico then go to San Dominigo and onto Jamaica.You can report the wreck of your ship there to the governor.i would like all the english men to be permanent members of my crew.yrs Captain Santos. The next week brought much activity aboard the sixty foot baracoon,as the holds were filled with cargo,then much more loaded on deck and tied down.Sugar cane and many barrels of rum,and fruit and vegetables of all types dried and fresh from local gardens.Simon told the captain they would stay on as crew after the reached Jamaica.So on hearing this two boxes of cuban cigars and four bottles of bourban were given to them by Jimbo the purser.All four pirate vessels left Antigua the next morning to raid ports around the caribean sea and tomurder and rape innocent victims.On the small clearing in front of his cave Toby was wasing a wahale bone,it was three feet long and intrically carved with scrimshaw. Toby said Yep young Willy done a smack up job on this here bone Binty,dont ya reckon matey.Bloody oath we taught him the craft of carvin like without us he would be buggered like a beached whale.said Binty This here bone tells a story of where all the gold bullion is and he said we have ta keep mum about the whole thing.Toby said.Sure it does the black clouds in the carving show the storm that wrecked Pinosa and killed all our crew .You can easy see poor old Grenoble smashed up on yon reef, and the sloop as was lost with all hands a sailing away on that fateful day,we can come back and collect the rest of the loot Toby said Binty Two boys walked up to the cave Charles Essex and Wally Meadows,good evening bosun can you show us how to make spears .We wish to do a spot of fishing to earn our keep as it were said Charles,Wally piped up and said,me knife is blunt,needs a bit of work on the stone like,to make it cut proper.Toby said binty get the sharpening stone from the cupboard beside you,and Charles use your machette to cut 4 six foot lenghts of bamboo.Binty took Charles away and taught him how to cut the bamboo,while Toby showed Wally how to sharpen any knife or sword on the stone with oil,As Wally worked on the edges of his knife blade Toby saw movement at sea and picked up his telescope . Sure enough there was Miguel Riouse the pirate Captain with his fleet of four vessels. Bloody hell he thought there be trouble coming,Wally go and get Willy tell him pirate ships sighted due west now be off ill finish your knife. Willy came back to the workshop what is so urgent Toby I have been catching lots of good fish for dinner .There be the black bastard pirate ships four of them,thirty two gun frigates sailing nor west past our island,bugger me what next .Toby said .Where did the ships come from,that is where the secret hideout is so we must prepare defences to protect the native villages .Lets see how much gunpowder and weapons we have and we can use the maps i made of pinosa .Wally said Charles can help you he has readin books on battles and wars,he saved in oilskins before the ship went down.Toby looked surprised at what Wally said and knew books cost a lot to buy .Where did he get them books Wally said Toby.Wally smiled and said his house in Essex is full of em Bosun,hundreds and more hundreds from the ground to the roof .His father is Lord of Essex a big high class bloke ya know what i mean.Bloody hell fire and brimstone,an Earl,s son lost on an island in the middle of the Carribee with pirates sailing and raiding,Jesus there will be hell to pay over this .The Earl will go right bonkers and give the Admiralty a right bollykin im sure said Toby.Willy said I do hope the lads in the cutter got to a safe port.The monsoon season starts this month and it is not safe to be at sea.Binty and Charles came back with a load of bamboo and berries they had picked in the jungle. All the fish and crabs were tossed into pots,the big kettle and small pots of yams hung over the fire .They ate and chatted about the pirates and helping the natives in time of danger.The five men went down the hill to the villages along the beach,to arrange a meeting with the full native council and there friend Nogoomo.Willy and his two native mates told the council of the pirate ships and what must be done to defend the villages against attack. Messages were sent all over the island with drums and three out riggers went to islands local islands to warn the Chiefs of pirate ships.The older men and women rested in the shade as most of the younger natives set to work,even the children joined in helping there mothers and fathers.They used fourty cannons brought ashore from Grenoble by the british crews months before hand.Trees were cut,bamboo vines and rocks were used to build walls that lent forward with spikes on top.These were coated with poison the natives used on the darts for the long deadly blowpipes .From the first day on landing ashore the british had taught the natives how to use all there weapons .Toby sorted them into groups of twenty men.half loading as the others fired there rifles,and bullets flew in all directions .The Chiefs prize rooster was shot and three pigs,until Toby stopped the firing practise. Binty took over and got the men to lie down and shoot at coconuts as targets well away from any native huts.after a while the natives could work as a team and keep up a steady rate of fire which was lethal.Five foot sharpened lengths of bamboo were set in the ground in deep trenches in front of the palisades walls then smeared with poison.Long tall walls were erected around every village on the island with all animals and food kept inside.All the creeks springs and rivers would be covered over if a pirate attack occured.Trenches were six feet in front of the walls and then shrubs covered them on slats of bamboo so when the pirates attacked they would fall in and die .A lookout was kept on the highest hill night and day to alert all of any pirate ships sighted .Stingray spurs,sharp bones and many more bones were bound to spears and arrows.. Small grenades made with coconuts and gun powder and steel bowls to have as braziers to light there fire arrows, A week a drum message was heard from Nando the island nearby. Three out riggers were seen rowing fast towards Pinosa The new arrivals told the men a pirate ship had attacked one of the largest villages and killed twenty natives, the kidnapped thirty five women . Willy was having a cup of tea when Owenga ran up to the shed and told him of the shocking deaths and what the pirates did on Nando island. Word spread fast and many people came up the hill to look through the telescope . Binty showed them how to use the glass resting on a tree fork to keep it steady Toby had seen three pirate ships a month ago and now he wondered where the other two ships had gone. Charles called out, there are the filthy swine, the sails and rigging is severely damaged and the bow has been smashed by gunfire. The Scorpion it reads on her stern plate has raided some port and was caught in the last storm said Willy. Toby had sent word for fifty natives all armed to the teeth, to assemble at the hut ready to fight.Right lets be havin the bastards tonight the lookouts have said the pirate ship is off the north coast.Lets sail in from seaward and steal there ship while they are attacking the the villages on shore he said.Jolly good show,we leave six hundred men ashore and take two hundred in your boats Toby said Willy. Binty how large is the Scorpion said Charles .It be a bloody rough sloppy three masted schooner about three hundred tons with black sails,with busted riggin gone ta hell.Thanks Binty you are now promoted to second leftenant,Toby is first and Charles is third rated .Wally Meadows be now a Bosun .Time for a toast to celebrate with Owenga,s guava juice what.The elder natives will be captains of each outrigger on the night raid as they know these waters best.From behind the defense walls chief Bowanga and his men waited then a creaking of rigging and the thud of a sail as it caught the wind.They be here said Billy Jenkins top gunners mate in charge .Yes big Toby he say wait until pirates knock on front door,bloody big bang Bowanga said and smiled Billy said young Owenga is way up in yon palm tree,and he signals with a small lamp then we fire.Make sure your men have plenty of fireballs for the catapults Chiefy.A row of cannons were set up in an arc,to cover the enimy,s approach form the beach to the walls.There sharp eyed spotters and message boys to inform the gunners where the best were.A few shaded lampthornes could be seen due north a sure sigm the pirates had began climbing down into there boats to row ashore.Women and children walked around with bags of powder and shot and food and water, for the men on guard at the walls A daring pincer movement had been planned to attack the pirates, from each end of beach were they would land ashore.Two hundred to hit both flanks and also from behind .Two long man pits had been dug from the walls to the beach either side .These had stakes set upwards on the bottom and sides,then hidden with wild shrubs.An hour later Billy saw a flicker of light and a bird call from Owenga in his tree.Five british crew lit the balls in the catapults,as the big native men pulled the ropes and woosh went the flaming balls.The first ball hit the ground sixty feet away and set the scrub alight amongst a line of rough dirty looking pirates. The fire balls shattered to pieces setting the pirates clothes on fire,as all the cannons opened up when a signal was given from the spotters.Two hundred and sixty pirates came ashore from the Scorpion,leaving only twenty on board to guard native hostages on the vessel.A large ragged line of screaming pirates charged the wall,with double axes,ladders maces and swords.Half of these were hit with poisoned darts from long blow pipes and musket shots from the high defence walls.Those who survived tried to stand the rough made ladders against the wall,and climb up.All of them fell through the shrubs onto the stakes to be skewered like pigs.Fifty pirates turned coward and headed back to there boats on the shore, as the cannon balls slaughtered many more.A fire arrow flew up from the right side of the beach and thunked into the wall,the signal from Nogoomo to stop the cannon fire.Then four hundred natives attacked the pirates from three sides at once After a long bloody battle the pirates had killed twenty two natives,but were overwhelmed by numbers.The natives stayed away and fired there crossbows and yew english bows from a safe distance,killing the pirates one by one.Eight pirates were captured alive and dragged to the main village. Wooden cages awaited them as per Toby,s orders,and the children at these devils with long sharpened bamboo rods.Out to seaward of the Scorpion Toby whispered to Willy in the boat next to his,you come in from the bow,real slow like be me comin up from the stern on the port side away from the beach.The crew aboard be dead keen ta see what be going on ashore.Send the natives over the deck rail first.Right and blacken your ugly big face cos they will spot you trait off said Willy. Laughing and yelling could be heard from the stern window as Toby,s boat passed by.Rimba a very strong small man was first up the anchor chain and over the rail.He saw three pirates drinking form jugs and gambling by small lanterns in the bow.He quietly crept along the deck rail and let down four rope ladders to his mates below.A pirate walked out of a cabin door onto the quarter deck and Rimba plunged his long dagger into his neck killing him.

The three pirates in the stern died quietly with there throats cut from ear to ear.Toby fired his musket to draw the pirates away from the women hostages.Captain Zangor heard the shot as he scoffed a bottle of brandy and he said to Belgan the the hunchback bosun see who fired that shot and kill them now.Then he went back to raping one of the native girls he had tied to the captains table. Toby shoved a long spear into Belgans guts as he attacked him with his sword and thirty natives went below decks.Captain Zangor was stabbed and beaten then tied up and put in the cages ashore with the other prisoners.Bowanga the chief had him tied to a tree and given two hundred lashes of the whip,then covered him in black pitch and set fire to him..A few days later Zangors body was mounted on a post, at the north headland as a warning to all pirates.The Scorpion vessel was cleaned and repaired and made ready for sea.A week long celebration followed and Willy took a sail to the four nearest islands,with lots of natives aboard so they could visit there many relations.Sir charles Weymouth the Governor of Jamaica sipped his large mug of morning coffee,with a small tote of rum to start his day.His large office had two wide windows with a superb view of Kingston harbour and he noticed a new ship sail into the bay.A baracoon leaning to port with all mainsails set,came flying into the bay swung to starboard took in some of her sails and gently edged up alongside the dock.The anchor dropped down and mooring ropes thrown to hands ashore.Damm good sailing Sir Charles thought and a yankee to by the colour of his flag,one wonders whom the captian may be.Simpson he called and refilled his mug from a large coffee pot.His senior aide arrived at a rush and said .How may the staff help you sir.I want you to whisk down to the dock in my coach and invite that yankee chap for dinner tonight what.He pointed at the baracoon at dock and handed Simpson a telescope he kept at hand who noticed the name of the ship on the stern plate. Simpson handed back the the glass and set off for the stables.Captain Santos was relaxing in a deck chair with his crew,under a large shade cloth rigged on between the masts.Mr simpson appeared at the dock next to the Red Fin in a white suit,red bow tie and wearing a panama hat,carrying a large umbrella. Ahoy there Red Fin he shouted.Simon Donald put his mug of bourbon on a barrel and strolled over to the deck rail and said .What be ya business here may I ask.Of course my man I come direct from the governors office mind to invite your captain to dinner this very night .Mr Bernard Simpson is my name young man.he said Come aboard matey,a toff ta see ya captain Simon said .Simpson lowered his umbrella and walked aboard and was led over to the men under the shade cloth.Danny me boy be so kind as to place a deck chair at our guests disposal Captian Santos said.Simon handed Simpson a glass of bourbon as Piere the chef arrived with two plates of canapes, and placed them on a card table.I have a french chef as my cook,saved him from a hanging in Puerto Rico,He was most grateful and decided to stay aboard as one of my crew.Costs me a dang fortune in wages,but he performs miracles in the galley if he gets the proper supplies.said the captain Danny Watson came back from the captains cabin with a log book and handed it to Simpson.On the first page at the top were the words The wreck of HMS Grenoble.Simon here and nine more of my crew are british seaman,and were aboard Grenoble when the ship hit a reef during a hurricane.This incident occured off Pinosa Island near Antigua and is my offical report .so hand it to the governor if you please.the captian said .Oh consider it done Captain,now I must get back to my duties with meal arrangements and so forth.Its been a pleasure to meet you sir said Simpson. He stood up,shook hands with the crew and made his way to the dock rather unsteady on his feet,after six glasses of bourbon.The governor had forgotten to have his afternoon tea.a most unusual occurence.Nimba the tea lady,was concerned about this shocking change of routine and said to Simpson,Is de boss sick has he got de gout or bad tummy Mr Simpson.No my dear do not fret so,all is well he is fully engrossed in reading a captains log book from the yankee ship just arrived..Yes sir I understand now said Nimba.Late in the day three well dressed men stepped down from an open horse drawn carriage at government house and entered the residence. Bimboo a huge six foot negro in a blue shirt, orange trousers and wearing a white top hat,barred there way .He politely asked there names the led them to the dining room.The Governor welcomed them personally and made introductions to his family and his eldest son Brian who was a captain in the navy .His vessel was the fourty two gun frigate Stingray which was docked with, the other two ships of the carribean squadron Condor and Raven. As a fine dinner of seafood and salads were consumed,with a selection of good wines young miss Petunia aged six said .Did you catch any naughty pirates on your last voyage sir.Oh my goodness yes we did miss Petunia we caught five of the ugly devils, and they had green eyes, and purple hair with big hooks in there ears and noses.I sold them for a florin each to a farmer in Santo Domingo. He hung them on posts to scare the birds away from his vegetable patches.Scarecrows is what the british call them.Miss Petunia put her hand over her mouth and giggled and everyone smiled.Simon Donald said we sighted four pirate ships in a small harbour at Antigua Sir Charles and were told the leader Captain Zangor is a vicious cut throat,without mercy and never takes prisoners.The black hearted swine is well known to me sir i assure you and many complaints have been made about his actions. An attack on the home base of these nest of vipers is paramount, and you can lead my squadron to there precise location the governor said to Simon. Take Simon and Danny with you as my ship sails for Florida within the week, and on my return i shall join your squadron at Landos bay the pirate hideout .The ten british crew went to fill out a admiralty report for the governor during the next week.At the same time on Pinosa Island Toby and Binty were in a heated argument about hiding the secret of the gold,and how to get it back to England. The work of many men for two months had produced fifty tons of gold in bags.I say we chuck it in now and hide what we has real sneaky like. said Toby.Bloody cods wallop to that caper we grabs the whole lot now,while the going is good. said Binty. Ya got birdshit for brains and what if we get caught red handed by yon navy loadin ta

Scorpion with the stolen loot .Them lads in the cutter may be havin afternoon tea an watercress sandwiches with the governor bugger me said Toby. You mean we comes back later for the rest you sly bastard,and where do we hide the bags aboard Toby.well i been lookin at them dooagrams in Willy,s books and a plan come to me see.We can take out twenty tons of ballast,load the loot in and put the ballast back on top.Whose to be knowin then Binty.The secret plan was started the next day and finished with the help of three hundred natives in three weeks .Just as well because a few days later Stingray and Redfin sailed through the entrance, in the reef.A formal meeting was held in a native long house with all involved with the wreck of the Grenoble present.Willy made a full spoken report and gave Captain Weymouth all the papers and logbooks he had collected from the wreck.He further informed the captain chief Bowanga had taken possession of the ship Scorpion after a battle with pirates.Also bowanga claimed salvage rights for the grenoble wreck under admiralty law.captain weymouth smiled and said.What would a native chief do with a pirate ship.Willy said Benson and Sykes Trading company has been formed and i am now a captain with a full crew in a private capacity .Here is my letter of resignation from the navy.The company will trade all over the carribean seas and with england.You have done well under such hardship and danger after losing most of your crew.charles essex and you were the only officers left to make any decisions .i shall duly report the situation in my diary and inform the governor of jamacia.He told them lord essex was sailing to kingston to find his son and an urgent lettter had been sent to tell him charles had been found alive and well. Willy told them he would sail for kingston for a letter of marque from the governor and to buy trade goods.were we at war with any nation at present he asked captain weymouth .spain and the netherlands were at war now so be wary of there ships at sea captain santos told him Toby gave the ten british crew of the redfin four chests,these had false floors with gold coins underneath and all were told to keep mum.On the voyage to kingston captain weymouth was aboard scorpion to teach willy and his crew tactics gunnery and ship handling methods.The three remaining pirate ships were destroyed at there hide out in the bay at antigua,after being unloaded of all cargo.charles essex returned to england with his father.Scorpion sailed for england and willy sent his crew to c hat with good friends and relations when the ship arrived. very soon two sloops docked at dichley farm on the dorset coast.the gold bags were taken from the boats in wagons under loads of of wood to barns,where they were hidden behind false walls. two years later another voyage to pinosa island with four new ships was made,and when three of them unloaded there cargo and departed .willy and his crew winched up the rest of the loot using the secret of the scrimshaw carvings on his whalebone .the exact location as you would find on the charts used by sir frances drake.captain santos bacame a partner in benson and sykes trading company and married a firey spanish beauty he met in mexico.toby and his two mates built a large township now the city of dorchester .binty built twenty seven inns throughout england now the dorchester hotels of england .the sons and daughters carried on with trading company business .in a nice big cottage in weymouth over the front door is a whalebone,on it is carved a wee poem .by three by four and many more.a secret never told,we took our chance,as we were bold .those lovely gold bags so full to hold . The end

The Captain's
Log Book

C aptain james willow,sipped a large balloon glass of brandy as he read slowly through a red leather bound log book.captain errol flynn was the author of the log book.a famous british navy commander well known,for his tactics.and actions at sea against arab pirates in africa. He had also captured or destroyed, many a vessel along the coast of india and ceylon.the pirates were always after richly laden merchant ships of any size,and there crews to capture and sell as slaves.captain flynn had captured or sunk one hundred and thirty two pirate vessels,during his long naval career and had only just retired to his estate in norfolk.james finished the last page of the log book and smiled,took a sip of brandy and closed the book.i shall take a ride,down to the docks to see if my three ships are ready to sail.he was a privateer,as were the other two captainsin the fleet,mr samuels and mr speaker all employed by mayfair shipping company.the owner,was lord baxton who had estates in suffolk and cambridge. there was fifteen ships in his fleet,and the bank of england had a third interest in the shipping company.james mounted his mare tuppence and rode down to morton docks and saw when he arrived bosun toms shouting loudly.a group of steverdores were loading a cutter,and the bosun said,pick up the pace,boyo,s this aint no tea party at the duke of cornwalls house ya know.morning bosun,is that the last boat load of supplies for my ship.how long to sailing time,i am most eager to depart.james said.noon be about right captain,and your dunnage has been placed in your cabin sir as ordered.said bosun toms james led his horse to harry.s stables,and gave young gem hopkins a gold sovereign to ride tuppence home for him.then he entered a eating house,the buttercup to order a roast beef,and all the trimmings.soon he was joined at table,by will evans his sailing master who chatted with james until it was time to board there ship,the tern.they were rowed out to the brigatine,in a jolly boat,and once aboard james did an inspection tour around the deck.he ordered the anchor up,and told the bosun to let go all sails,except the top gallants. the pilot had the helm.the schooner dragon,and the sloop sea gull were in line astern as the three ships sailed down the west coast of africa on route to cape town.only one incident had occured so far,off the coast of sierra leon when five arab dhows were sighted to port just on dusk.an preplanned strategy for this type of action,was carried out now,the first two vessels reduced sail,while the schooner veered to port and closed the dhows from behind.captain speaker in command ordered the gunners,to fire several broadsides to port and starboard,as his ship charged through the centre of the small arab fleet. he sank one dhow,and set fire to another and the pirates scuttled for there home base ashore.the three ships docked at cape town,and the three captains went ashore,to the british embassey.all the ships were unloaded of english trade goods.timber,spices and gold were purchased and loaded.james bought a large stock of diamonds from,the de beer company. these stones were packed in boxes marked ladies perfume and condiments, for security reasons.at the embassey mr smythe jones the ambassador informed them,quite a few ships had been captured,along the east coast of africa.some vessels had been sunk or set fire too,the crews being held for ransom or sold into slavery.the evil bastard,the sultan of zanzibar and his pirate rabble,were causing all these problems at sea.there was many native slavers also,ashore in league with the pirates.a oweek later saw,the british ships dock at port elizabeth,for two days then on to durban to load native artefacts and woven goods.bosun toms and james were sipping ale,at the three bells tavern and over heard a conversation.a major of marines said to a friend,the sheik zayal bin shamon,has declared war on the sultan of zanzibar,cos his two daughters were kidnapped from his large dhow the falcon. and damn me, one thousand gold rials is the reward for knowledge of his daughters exact whereabouts. he has promised to burn at the stake,all those involved in such a henious crime.two nights later,the english ships were anchored close in shore,in a small bay. With hardly a sound one hundred natives,had swum from canoe,s and climbed aboard the dragon.the five guards on deck were killed by arrow,s or had there throats cut. A bird call,was a signal for the rest of the mixed crew to paddle up and board the schooner.three french officers took charge,and ordered all sails set and made a course for the zabezi river mouth.timmy dobbs,was the lookout on board the sea gull,and had just came on deck,to start his watch.he grabbed his telescope and, he noticed the sails unfurl on the dragon,and raced down to wake captain samuels. the captain staggered on deck still half asleep,and it took some time,for him to find out what happened.a boat was sent to the tern,to inform captain willow of the stolen vessel.both ships weighed anchor and set off in pursuit of the dragon. there was no sign of the dragon ahead,so the two ships headed for a wide river mouth and sent a boat ashore.the crew asked the local natives if they had seen a ship sail pass.the big headman told the crew, a large canoe with bat wings had passed up river in the night,like an owl with no sound.the crew gave him an axe,flour sugar and a few bags of seeds, they thanked the headman,and returned in there boat to inform the capatain of there news.as a lunch of cheese and fresh fruit was enjoyed aboard tern,a large fleet of sixteen dhows and two frigates appeared from the north.the two frigates were,the signet and the vulture and the vulture heaved to and dropped anchor.the signet sailed close to the tern,and came about,then dropped her sail,s smartly and dropped her hook.the second frigate vulture heaved to nearby.all of the arab dhows and the two frigates,flew a bright yellow flag with a green star. this was the flag of sheik zayala abin shamon,the ruler of vast lands to the north of africa.a small dhow came, alongside to deliver a message for james which invited him and five officers to dinner aboard signet.a cutter was rowed to the arab frigate,and the six men went aboard.james noticed several white men, amongst the crew and wondered why they were aboard. Sheik shamon was standing proudly by the helm,with a young boy of twelve,beside him and an older boy a replica of himself on the other.there were two,young girls in arab dress,behind the sheik wearing veils on there faces.raji shamon,the young boy,stepped forward, he was dressed in a english midshipman,s uniform and saluted captain willow and said.good afternoon sir,my name is raji,my father thanks you kindly,for accepting his invitation to dine with us.we have lost my sister,s and there friends from there ship the falcon, which was captured by evil pirates along this coast.your father will get your sisters back,who is the other boy beside your father,midshipman raji.said capt,willow.the boy is jayman,my big brother and he and father do not speak good english.please have patience at dinner captain as i translate the conversation for you,raji said.of course raji,tell your father i have many arab friends and understand,the customs and culture of your tribes.a small boy,malosh the cooks assistant came out of the captains cabin and spoke to raji.then he returned to the galley.raji said,dinner is served please join us at table.james and his men entered the large cabin,to find many dishes laid out on small tables.bowls of scented water,were handed to guests with towels to wash and dry there hands.half an hour later.the sheik spoke in rapid arabic to raji.the two arab girls chattered together and spoke to there father.there was a waving of hands,bows and gestures,then everyone relaxed.raji said my father asks for your knowledge and experience to assist in the rescue of his daughters and the twenty ladies of the harem.

the evil dogs of pirates,may keep them as wives or sell them as slaves at zanzibar. He asks why your ships are here,near the mouth of the zimba river. james replied i have three ships.the settlers and most of the crew of the schooner dragon,were ashore hunting game.or collecting fruit and herbs. dragon was captured,and sailed inland by the zimba at night.we shall join forces raji and wipe out the hyena.s of the coast,say this to your father lad. more discussion occured and the sheik ordered two of his aides,to bring a chest of documents.he handed two scrolls to raji,who gave them to james.the first document read.this is a letter of marque,which entitles the holder to raid and destroy all pirates at sea or on land along the length of the coast of africa.signed sheik zayala shamon .raji said sir james you are now an admiral in my fathers navy,as i told him a captains rank is mere poppycock yes and smiled.i think,i am right in this.the second document is a contract,to share the profits of all goods we capture from the pirates.my father recieves 60%and you 40% as he has more men and ships. please sign the documents as agreed admiral willow.

which james did,and handed the documents back to raji who said, my father employed an english tutor,mr knox to teach me admiralty law,and sailing matters of importance.well raji so far mr knox,has done a fine job,but you need practical experience aboard my ship the tern.ask jayman to join us too,it will be good training for the sons of sheik shamon.after speaking with his father,this transfer was agreed to and all present discussed different plans to rescue the ladies.will evans the sailing master,had the best plan,forty british crew would go ashore in light chains.one hundred arabs acting as slave traders would go inland to sell there slaves,captured from a ship.a normal routine all along the coast of africa.the sloop sea gull had a shallow draft so would lead the signet upriver.four small dhows went ahead to check, both sides of the river for any danger.signet stayed back,until more fire power was called for if problems arose.the rest of the english and arab vessels .patroled up and down the coast .james on the sea gull,s quarter deck,spotted smoke far ahead and asked captains jenkins to heave too.then send two armed cutters ahead.these boats had thirty men and two carronades in the bow.ben davis quarter master and sharif went ashore with sixty men,and found the slave camp.as planned an hour later.bashra the arab slave trader,led his white captives into the camp.he spoke with camp leader hammid,who said tie the white dogs to trees near the river,we shall drink and enjoy the woman.we shall put them,in the stockade later.bashra,s men took the british men out of site and gave them arms and keys to the chains.sharif sent four men,to scout the whole area,before he made any attack.there was shouting and screaming heard in the distance,and ben davis led his men forward to meet the scouts.they rushed to the river and attacked twenty drunken men,who were raping the women slaves.sharif arrived too,and all the men were killed.only fifteen guards were,on duty at the stockade,and most were drunk,the arabs slit there throats and the british shot any who tried to escape. the slaves were all released,a nd taken to the river to wash,then loaded aboard the seagull to rest and sleep.the camp was searched,and destroyed then a much wider check was made along jungle trials.

three slavers were kept alive,and sharif used hot iron bars to torture them for six hours.after the truth was found out,the three men were fed to the crocidiles.another slave camp was one hundred and fifty, miles up the coast at marques an old french port.twenty five bags of gold were,found in a cave near the slave camp.many more tons,of ivory and gold were,sent from marques by dhows to a bay close by.the loot and slaves went to zanzibar and the gross fat sultan,the lowest filthy dog in africa. the sheiks daughters zeno and bamon,and the rest of the harem ladies were safe,and back aboard the signet.seagull and signet came about and headed for the open.sea.five fast zaraqs sailed north to find the bay,the slavers spoke about.six ships entered the bay of mitanbe,where six hundred men went ashore. twelve hundred slaves were released,after a three hour fight with arab slavers.the bodies piled in heaps and burnt.three tons of gold nuggets and powder was found,and sixty elephant tusks in three caves near the camp.next the fleet sailed for marques,with three swift faraqus to sail ahead and investigate the bay at marques.the crew were to land at a small inlet and climb to a high hill on a headland,then send a report by pigeon messenger to captain willow aboard the tern.two of the local natives had informed the crew of seagull,that the dragon ship sailed inland along the zambesi river to marques with native pilots who knew the sand bars and shoals well.raji and jayman were using a five foot telescope on a tripod,to survey the marques huge slave camp below.four thousand slaves wite and black were in large stockades,gaurded by two hundred men.five germans and twenty frenchmen were in command of the camp,and lived in sixteen native huts two miles from the camp.ten arab crew from the the faraqu vessel zaba returned four hours later and told raji about all the details of the slave camp.jayman slipped a message,on saladin his big pigeon and let him loose.sheik shamon was sipping earl gray tea,with captain willow when flew in and landed in his coup.the dhow captain,sharif camled the bird and talked to him as he slipped the message of his leg.and gave him fresh water and feed.sharif sat down next to sheik shamon,and gave him the message which he read,as he studies charts of the coast laid open on a large table.sharif translated the arab written message from,raji fro captain willow.s benefit and james made many notes with quill and ink.the german swine have twenty four sixteen pound cannons.there is three batteries of eight cannon,s at the rear,and on each side of the bay.any ship entering marques bay will be blown to hell,from three directions sharif,said captain willow.did the ship dragon have these cannon,s aboard when the vessel was captured and sailed upriver captain,said sharif. Yes sharif the cannons have been taken ashore to set up a defence,for the slave camp against any ememy vessels.said captian willow.a long discussion continued for three hours,then dinner was served aboard signet.a three pronged attack,was decided upon.first the Huts and the battery of cannons nearby controlled by the white men,must be captured,on the north side of the bay.these cannon were to be turned and sighted on the west battery.the south battery to be captured,and fire directed on the west battery,as four hundred men killed the guards and released the slaves from the stockades.six small faraqus would sail around the bay firing at will at all enemy targets and assist any escaping slaves.the whole fleet of allied ships arrived in the dark of night,below the headland where raji was stationed,and vulture and seagull sailed on to disembark five hundred men on the south side of the bay. The forty men at the huts were garroted or stabbed and two germans were shot with small pistols.these men were experts inartillery and had to be killed.the cannons were turned the range set. sharif and bazaka a huge man set fire to the four german and french native huts,after putting barrels of gunpowder underneath each hut,the fuses were lit and each hut exploded.ten men escaped to run for the bay,but were caught by freed salves from the stockade, who hacked them to death and threw there bodies in the sea for the crabs sharks and barracuda to eat.five hundred british crew men shot and burned on a huge fire the two hundred guards,then attacked the west battery of cannons from the jungle behind them.they stood and gave the men at the cannons thirty shots of continuous fire,until all were dead.all papers.gold and ivory was collected from one hundred miles around the camp.three white men were found captain james van der veen,and his two bosun.s the huge amit pandey and murali kemati his quartermaster also the midshipman ayush sinha who had been captured by captain salazar .these men had sailed in the fastest clipper ghandi made in madrass of the finest timbers by the best shipwrights the master craftsmen of ship building.the british were shown to be complete fools in all forms any type of indusrty of any kind.captain willow sent two cutters back down the zambesi river,and the ghandi was found tied to several trees by ropes.the crews from the cutters boarded and sailed the vessel back. two months passed before forty tons of gold and six hundred tusks of ivory were loaded aboard the fleet.the vulture and took all the slaves back to port elizabeth.zamboo the local native zulu cheif arrived and had a meeting with raji and jayman.raji took zamboo and four warroir,s to his father by boat the signet .zamboo spoke to namimba captian speakers bosun a zulu tribes man zamboo told the story,of six villages raided by french men who took 10000 of my native men and women over the last five years.these captives were taken by ship to zanzibar,by order of the fat pig of a sultan.sheik shamon listened to raji,as he told the story of from the zulu cheif. then he ordered three hundred zulu,warriors to come aboard his fleet of ships.we sail now to for zanzibar and mombasa to destroy the slave trade along the east coast forever.the dragon and the ghandi,were repaired and made ready for sea.The fleet of six frigates and fifty,dhows sailed north for zanzibar.james willow,ayusha raji and jayman were in the captain,s cabin,looking at a chart of dar el salaam harbour.jayman pointed his dagger at a spot on the chart,and spoke in rapid arabic to raji. captain willow my bother jayman has sailed,many times into this bay with my father,s trading fleet. he says the sands,shift with the currents,and after a large storm,many large vessels have run aground. the stupid captains,do not use small,boats to check the depth before the enter harbour.they also refuse to pay for a pilot to guide them in safely.they act like,the big bull charging at the gate,yes that is what mr knox told me,said raji.good lad jayman and bosaun of the dutch merchant ship burgen,told us of bad hurricanes from mombasa to zanzibar.yes i remeber the big fat man with,the red hair and funny hat on, he shouted like an elephant,raji said. the next day a fifty foot pirate baglash,was captured by signet with thirty men aboard.sheik shamon ordered all the men beheaded, and the bodies thrown over board.a small crew was put on the vessel with thirty barrels of gunpowder,and would be used as a fire ship during the coming attack on zanzibar.sea gull and the tern,sent two cutter,s into the harbour amongst five dhows of the sheiks fleet. the vessels stayed in port,for three days then returned to the signet for a meeting to plan there next move against the sultan.the dragon and the ghandi frigates captured six more pirate vessels and these were loaded with oil and gunpowder.a week later twenty dhows sailed slowly into dar el salaam harbour,and when no hazards were found a flag signal was sent to the frigates out at sea.eight dhows were set alight and the helms locked to direct them towards large ships moored along the docks,the two men crews jumped into small canoes and were picked up by sheik shamons dhows.the tern and dragon shelled fort harid o an island in the centre of the harbour for four hours,wrecking all the cannons and the powder store.vuture signet and ghandi sailed around the harbour,smashing all the palace buildings along the shore.seagull backed up,the fire of the dhows,as they destroyed one ship after another.five large dhows,tried to escape but tern and dragon blew them to pieces with,heavy broadsides from port and starboard guns.all the sheiks fleet sailed out of the harbour at dusk to a small inlet.four more attacks were made and twenty more pirate vessels captured,the they sailed due north raiding many islands along the way.a month later saw the combined fleet tied up at the sheiks home port of ethiopia.a long celebration was held and hundreds of wagons, were used to transport all the loot to the treasury.all the crews went ashore to bathe and change,into clean arab robes and have an english morning tea of kippers and toasted sandwiches.then raji euniches and many veiled ladies took a tour of dubhouli city and a cruise down the river in small dhows.the british crews sat back and enjoyed the festivities,as they were fed fresh fruit and native guava.many such tours occured over the next six months,by camel and on horseback across the sheiks vast country.six arab horses were given to the three british captians to breed and race in england.these would be put aboard before there ships sailed home.piere the french chef from the tern caused quite a huge,interest at the palace when he was given a large kitchen and eighty men to cook regular meals.the sheik and most of the ladies adored french food and the many sauces created,to go with each dish.fifty men and women were put to work finding all the varied ingredients needed for his culninary delights.the english ships sailed for home,after a six months stay in ethiopia with samboo the sheiks daughter now mrs willow.her two sisters and four arab body guards accompanied her on the voyage.the vessels set sail for capetown to sell the pirate loot captured on there raids.it took two weeks for repairs and restocking water and fresh food,then the mayfair ships sailed for england. Raji and ayusha had been the match makers in this relationship,telling wild stories of all kinds about capatain willows.his daring actions,against five men at once slaying them all with his rapier,and many more outrageous tales.a week after docking his fleet at plymouth,captain james willow went to a meeting with lord baxton at whites club in london.when the two men,were seated with drinks,lord baxton said,you have done a damn fine job on your last voyage me lad,one hundred thousand pounds profit.here are some documents for you to sign,which i had my barrister draw up.read them first of course, and sign if you agree to the terms. in a nutshell you now own a one third share of mayfair shipping company,and the profits from your future voyages will be divided in your favour. you shall recieve sixty percent .and myself forty percent as i obtain huge trade profits from my fleet of ships.thanks berty i shall return to africa in one months time,and mrs willow has invited your family to my house in oxford for the weekend.from africa i must go to pinda near calcutta to carry out a duty of honour for captain errol flynn my uncle. the sheik,s six new sloops will sail with me,and two hundred tons of wood and other supplies he ordered as well said captain willow.berty baxton said two navy frigates,will escort you back to africa.the admiralty want this slavery business wiped out. admiral hood advised me,last week he will be sending a dozen more navy vessels,to patrol our shipping lanes.the two went into the dining room,to enjoy a large pheasent with fresh cooked vegetables each,then cheese and cognac later.lord baxton gave james a parchment,with all the names of the capatains and crew of the frigates gannet and eagle. these ships had been repaired and returned to service,after action in the battle of trafalgar.just on dawn a month later,two french frigates,attacked the sea gull,which had sailed inshore chasing a small pirate baluga vessel.the seagull charged at the stern of liberty,and raked the rear cabins with hot shot. In a very short time four ships surrounded the two french frigates.the navy frigates dismasted la force and damaged liberty.dragon and tern,came along side la force and threw grappling ropes.the sharp shooters shot most of the officers and the crew surrended.liberty did the same when they saw the fellow french ship yield.all the french crews were put ashore on the ivory coast and the fleet sailed on to cape town with there two prizes.a spanish ship had been sunk off,the coast of morocco after fifteen english navy slaves had been found aboard,the spanish crew were locked in the hold to drown with there ship as it went down.captain salazar recieved two hundred lashes and was thrown over board as shark bait.the mayfair fleet sailed on,collecting trade goods for india and arrived in bombay.the tern unloaded first,and set sail for pinda a little above madras. James sat at his captains table,making navigation positiions in lattitude and longditude while he made reference to a chart of the east indian coast.he was tracing,the course taken by captain errol flynn,six years ago to find the crew of a british navy vessel.twenty two leagues north,of madras he would find the palace of rajah nayanka,a traitorous murdering bastard soon to meet shame and the cruelest form of death.inside the fat ugly swines quarters,were four hundred chests of opium.and twenty large boxes of rough daimonds.these goods and many more had been stolen,from the frigate kimberely at madras harbour.

an irish cook aboard the vessel,had taken a bribe of
two hundred gold coins from an indian he met at
a tavern.he was supplied with herbal drugs to put
in the food and ale,then let a gang of thugee.s
aboard who murdered all the crew.the bodies of all
the british crew,and sailed the kimberly to a small
inlet up the coast at pinda.ten british crew returning
from hospital had seen the kimberly sail away.then
they found the bodies of the crew in the water and
stole a dhow.they followed the ship to a wharf at
pinda and returned to madras reporting to the
consul at the british embassy.captain flynn was
informed by the admiralty later of his son,s body
found slashed and eaten by fish and crabs.he was
thirty years old and captain of the kimberly.the log
book told,how captain flynn and a dozen of his
negro crew disguised themselves and went
ashore,from his frigate onslow.they scoured the
waterfront and with bribes and threats found four
of rajah nayanka,s men feasting like pigs at a brothel
in madras.his men bound and gagged the four
indian men and took them by coach to his ship.
each man was strapped over,a cannon and given

twenty lashes and questioned about the murders. no one said a word,so benson the quartermaster had three hands winch a large tub,and a thirty foot wooden box up from number one hold.bloody hell, ta captain has got big bertha out,these thugee,s be curtains now said middy simon ward to his friend leftenant barrows.very true they will spill there guts now mind.said the leftenant.benson opened the long box with a crowbar and picked up one of the indians and dropped him in the box.a twenty five foot anaconda,becomes very angry indeed when woken from a peaceful sleep.and even more so when the snake is hungry.the other three indians were,dragged foward to see what would happen to there thugee comrade.bertha bit a large chunk of flesh out of sinbads neck,as she wrapped her body several times aound him,and started to squeeze.his three indian friends felt very scared and sick,as they watched in horror and heard sinbad scream his guts out.then abdul started begging for mercy as he told the real story of the raid on the kimberly.captain flynn made certain,all the names of those involved was written down.he vowed revenge on the rajah nayanka in the future.the tern was met by nepal a big dhow,at a cove near pinda.six small tough looking men came aboard by boat from the vessel,and captain willow shook hands with each of his uncles and cousins.they all had a dinner in the captains cabin,sitting on the floor,as was there native custom.piere put on a excellent array of dishes,and soups.the men in the dhow were ghurka.s a fierce tribe of deadly warriors from nepal,who were so quiet on there feet,they could creep upon one without a sound.if you were an enemy,a small razor sharp knife a kukri would slit your throat is a second.terak the leader of the ghurka,s told a tale of heavy taxes,raids pillage and murder by the rajah,s men into many countries for the last two years.he must be destroyed and robbed of all his wealth. I shall take my share,the rest to be returned to those he raided.said captain willow. benson knocked and entered the captains cabin, with four crew men.they placed boxes and leather bags on the floor,and left the cabin.james had spent ten years of his life,among many friends in the mountains of nepal.his father had been,a colonel in the army there and had recently retired.these are gifts for for you and the elders terak,open them and see what i brought from england for you.namuk was the first to,open a cedar box and took out a new mauser rifle and looked at it closely.in the box was a long black painted telescopic sight to fit for long range sniping shots.other ghurka.s opened fine folding leather bags to find kukri,s of all sizes and belts to slip them in for battle.these were custom made by wilkinson sword company.james said i have fifty tons of rifles and ammunition,plus more sets of knives to protect you against all enimies terak,thank you james,we need these weapons urgently.now we shall plan an attack on the rajah,s palace.six cutters and the nepal sailed down nagpur river at night,to the rear of the rajah,s palace at pinda.thirty ghurka,s melted silently away to check the entrances and guard system.zha min returned within the hour,to say twenty guards on the walls are dead and thirty more captured and locked up.an old white haired man had come with zha min who was the palace mason.he had informed terak of two secret doors,one which led too the treasure room and the other led to the river.most of the army had gone north to raid howrah.all the british crews went through the whole palace,from top to bottom,the huge fat pig rajah nayanka was found,with six girls and two young boys.benson heated up a sabre on a brazier and jabbed him in the arse then burnt all his hair off.he was doused in water,tied up and sent to the river.a palace guard showed them the treasure room and the secret tunnels.terak took his share down to four dhows his men had captured.captain willow sent fifty wagons of gold and coins to the local village council to be shared equally amongst all the citizens.a week later the tern sailed south,and piere the chef poisined the rajah with doses of arsenic.and shoved a pigs foot in his mouth.timkins the ships carpenter made a coffin for the rajah in the shape of a pig,and painted it bright red.at a muslim mosque near madras the crew dumped the coffin at the front door and left.captain willow learned at cape town,the british navy had attacked zanzibar in force and killed the sultan and most of his men.his ship docked for a week and then sailed home for england.james willow retired from sea duties when he returned to england,and the coach with him and gem arrived at parmsley his oxford house. samboo his wife came,running down the front steps,with june seymour her maid who had a baby in her arms.after captain willow kissed his good lady,on the cheek he said.now my dear whose is this little chap.the maid took a little book from her pocket,and handed it samboo who smiled and said my dear sir may i present captain thomas nelson willow junior,and this is his log book,it is up to date as you can see his thumb print on the first page.the book was light blue,with a little sailing ship on the front.at the top of the book in gold letters the title read,---ADMIRALTY ORDERS FOR YOUNG NAVY CAPTAINS UNDER FIVE YEARS OLD. THE END .april 7th 5,20 pm

Printed in the United States
By Bookmasters